This annual
belongs to

....

....

EGMONT
We bring stories to life

First published in Great Britain 2014 by Egmont UK Limited,
The Yellow Building, 1 Nicholas Road, London W11 4AN

Written by Laura Green
Designed by Clare Yeo and Cassie Benjamin

HiT entertainment

ISBN 978 1 4052 7206 3
57513/2
Printed in Italy

Stay safe online. Any website address listed in this book are correct
at the time of going to print. However, Egmont is not responsible
for content hosted by third parties. Please be aware that online
content can be subject to change and websites can
contain content that is unsuitable for children.
We advise that all children are supervised
when using the internet.

Adult supervision is recommended
when glue, paint, scissors and
other sharp points are in use.

CONTENTS

Meet the Emergency Crew! 8

Meet the Pontypandy Friends! 10

Bessie to the Rescue! 12

Colour Time! 18

Odd One Out 19

Spot and See 20

Battle of the Birthdays 22

Count Along with Mandy 28

Always on Duty! poster 29

Sam to the Rescue poster 30

Rescue at Sea 31

Wheel·y Fun with Paint! 32

3,2,1 ... Blast Off! 34

Blazing Maze! 35

Nee Nah! Nee Nah! 36

New Friends in Pontypandy! 38

Ben to the Rescue 39

Charlie's Boat 40

Norman's Snow Go! 42

Best Sleepover Ever! 44

Red Alert! 50

Kite Colour 51

Spot the Difference 52

Pencil Ready 54

Shadow Match! 55

Eye Spy 56

The Pontypandy Polar Bear 58

Quiz Time! 64

See You Soon! 66

Answers 67

MEET THE EMERGENCY CREW!

Fireman Sam

Fireman Sam is always ready to drive Jupiter to an emergency. You can count on Sam to save the day!

Penny

Penny uses Neptune the lifeboat for emergencies at sea. She drives Venus the rescue tender when there's trouble on land.

Tom Thomas

Tom flies his helicopter, Wallaby One, to mountain rescues!

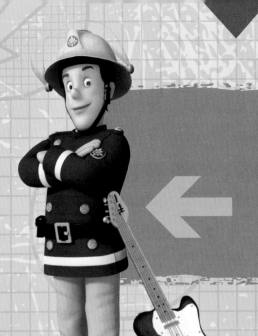

Elvis

Elvis is a tip-top firefighter, who always lends a hand. He secretly dreams of being a pop star too!

Station Officer Steele

Station Officer Steele runs the Pontypandy Fire Station. He likes things to be just right.

Radar

Radar the rescue dog can sniff out trouble anywhere. **WOOF! WOOF!**

MEET THE PONTYPANDY FRIENDS!

Dilys and Norman Price →

Dilys and **Norman** live above their shop. When Naughty Norman isn't causing trouble, he helps his mum out.

← The Flood Family

The Floods live in a little cottage in Pontypandy. **Mike Flood** is a handyman but he's always having accidents! **Mandy** is Norman's best friend.

The Jones Family →

Charlie Jones is a fisherman and his wife **Bronwyn** runs the Wholefish Café. **Sarah** and **James** love eating lunch in their mum's café. Yum!

Gareth Griffiths

Gareth lives and works at the Mountain Railway Station. He makes sure the Pontypandy Flyer is on time!

Trevor Evans

Trevor drives his friends all over Pontypandy in his bus!

Moose Roberts

Moose runs the Mountain Adventure Centre. His best friend is Tom and they like to be called The Wild Men of Pontypandy! They are real explorers!

BESSIE TO THE RESCUE!

Fireman Sam and Officer Steele were about to do a safety inspection at the Railway Station. Officer Steele's first fire engine used to run on the railway line many years ago!

Officer Steele soon stumbled across an old shed.

Inside, was his fire engine – Bessie! She was very dusty and dirty.

"I can't let anyone see you like this, Bessie!" he whispered, and he quickly closed the door.

Fireman Sam finished the inspection. The station passed with flying colours.

"Next stop – Mountain Activity Centre!" said Sam, hopping onto the Pontypandy Flyer.

"Erm, you go ahead. I've got something to do here ..." said Officer Steele.

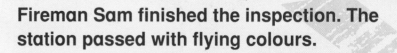

As soon as the Flyer pulled out of the station, Officer Steele pushed Bessie out of the shed.

Sarah and James couldn't believe their eyes when they saw the old fire engine!

"This is Bessie. She's not looking her best," Officer Steele sighed. "Would you like to help me clean her up?"

"Yes, please!" James and Sarah said, grabbing a bucket and sponge.

At the Mountain Activity Centre, Moose was busy cooking sausages on a campfire.

"Fancy a sausage?" Moose asked, when Sam and Gareth pulled up in the Flyer.

"Thanks Moose, but I've got an inspection to do!"

Back at the Railway Station, Sarah, James and Officer Steele scrubbed, brushed and washed every last part of the old engine.

Soon, Bessie was sparkling!

"Wow!" said James. "She's as good as new."

"It's a shame she's not needed anymore," said Officer Steele.

At the Mountain Activity Centre, things weren't running quite so smoothly. Moose had dropped some empty gas canisters into the campfire!

"Stand back!" said Fireman Sam. "If there's any gas inside, they could explode!"

Sam quickly phoned the Fire Station. He needed back up – and fast!

Penny and Elvis raced to the Railway Station first. They needed to take the fire equipment up the mountain in the Pontypandy Flyer. It was too steep for Jupiter.

But when they arrived, Officer Steele told them the Flyer was already up the mountain!

Oh dear!

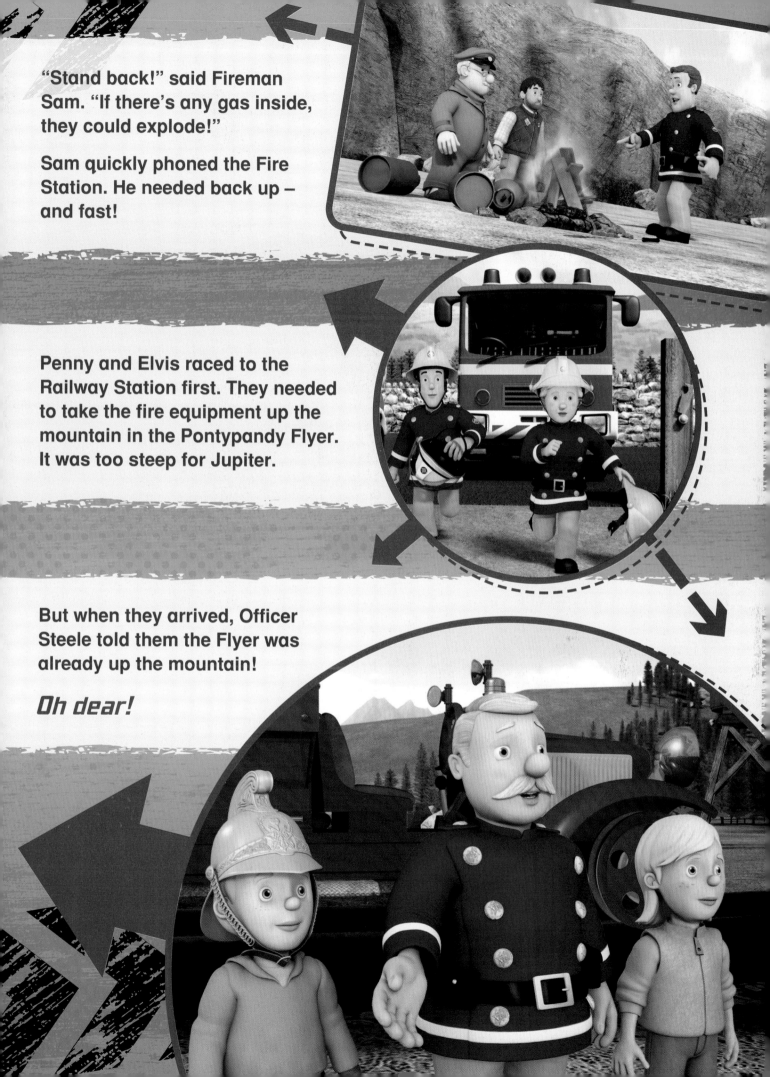

Then Officer Steele had an idea.

"Let's take Bessie!" he said.

He slowly turned Bessie's crank handle ... the engine spluttered and then roared into life!

"Are you sure she'll make it?" asked Penny, frowning.

"I know she will," said Officer Steele.

Bessie was soon packed up and ready to roll!

Officer Steele and Bessie raced up the mountain.

"Just like the old days, Bessie! Ya-hoo!"

Fireman Sam got a surprise when Bessie pulled up! But he quickly got to work.

Sam unravelled the hose and water shot out of the nozzle. The flames soon died down.

Bessie had saved the day!

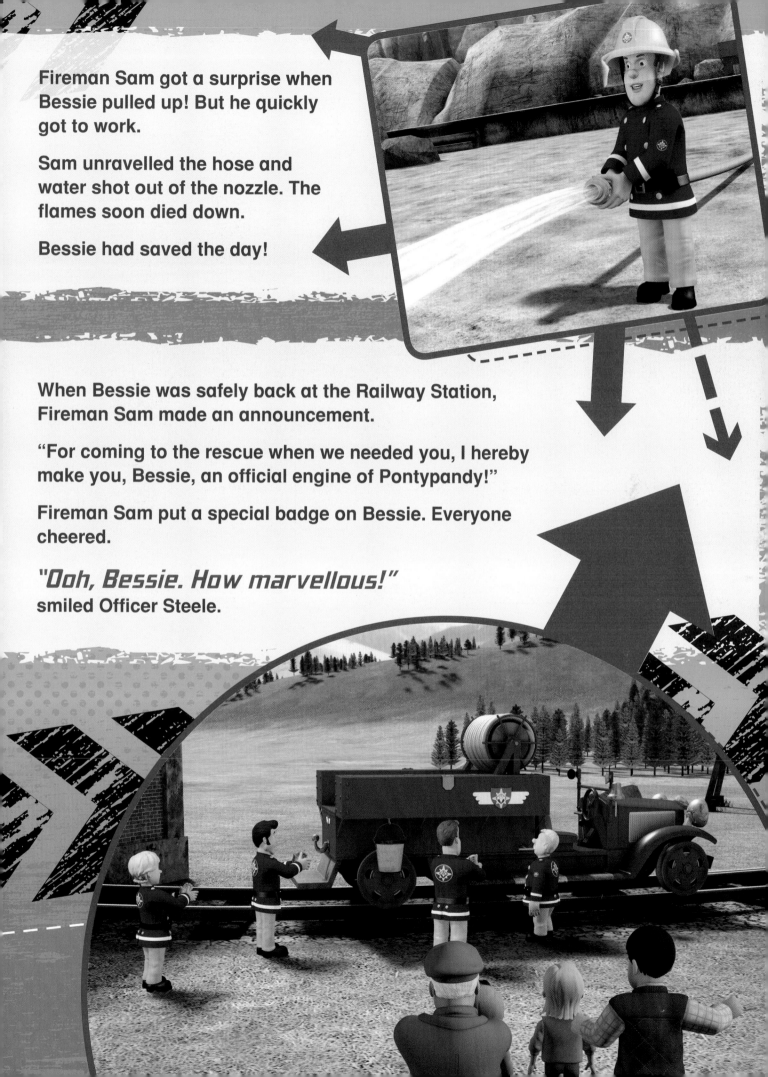

When Bessie was safely back at the Railway Station, Fireman Sam made an announcement.

"For coming to the rescue when we needed you, I hereby make you, Bessie, an official engine of Pontypandy!"

Fireman Sam put a special badge on Bessie. Everyone cheered.

"Ooh, Bessie. How marvellous!" smiled Officer Steele.

COLOUR TIME!

Use your **BRIGHTEST CRAYONS** to colour in this big picture of Fireman Sam swinging to the rescue!

ODD ONE OUT

There are lots of interesting animals in Pontypandy. Can you spot the odd animal out in each row?

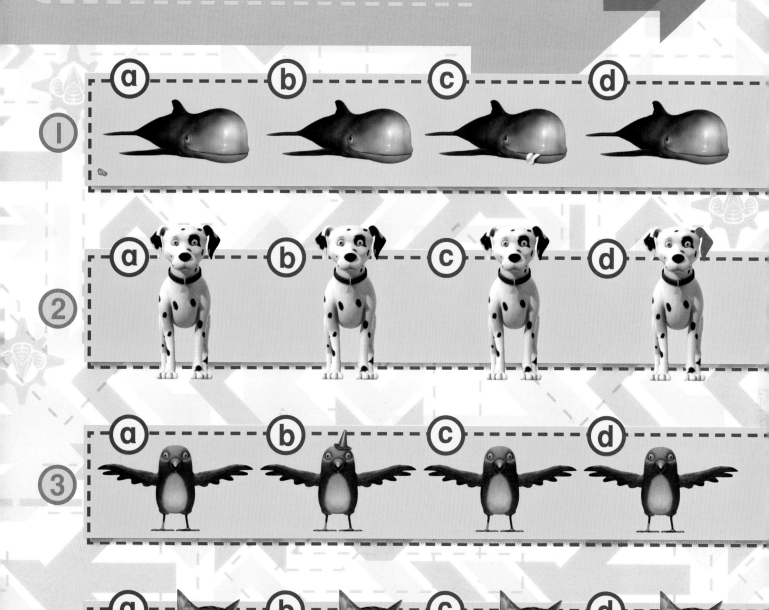

Answers on page 67.

SPOT AND SEE

There's an emergency at the lighthouse! Look carefully at this rescue scene to find the objects on the opposite page!

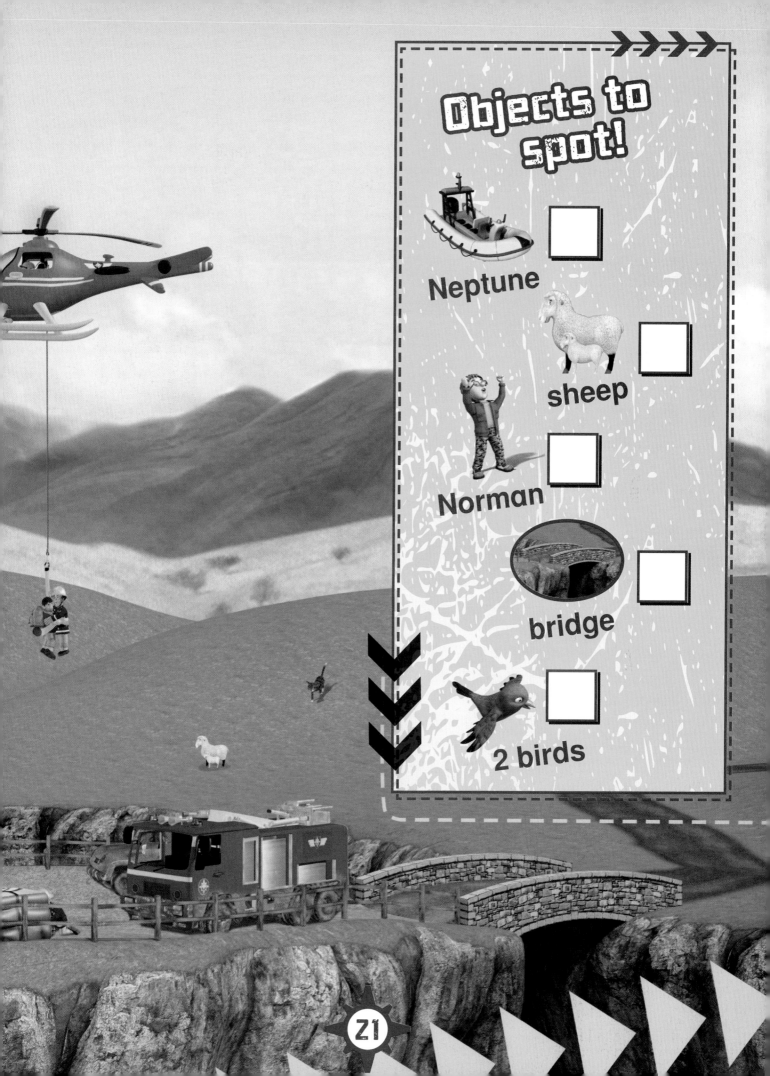

Objects to spot!

Neptune ☐

sheep ☐

Norman ☐

bridge ☐

2 birds ☐

21

BATTLE OF THE BIRTHDAYS

It was James and Sarah's birthday and this year, they were having their own parties.

"My football party will be better than your science party!" said Sarah.

"No way! Science is best!" said James.

At the Fire Station, volunteer firefighters were learning about fire extinguishers. But Trevor kept forgetting which extinguisher was used for which fire.

Luckily, Elvis was on hand to sing a tune ...

Red is for wood, cream is foam, black is for liquid, take care in the home!

Meanwhile, Sarah's football party was in full swing! All the children were doing keepy-ups and headers.

"This is a *brilliant* party!" said Norman.

Next it was James' turn for his science party. But his party didn't go quite to plan.

Nobody was interested in Mrs Chen's experiments – so they all ran back to Sarah's football party!

"Is there anything more exciting you could do?" asked James. "Like make a rocket or a robot with laser eyes?"

Mrs Chen knew just the trick to bring the children back to the party.

When James had gathered his friends again, Mrs Chen began the experiment.

"If you pour sodium into water, it'll make fire," said Mrs Chen.

Sure enough, the water burst into flames!

SMASH!

Just then, Sarah kicked a ball outside. It flew through the window ... and smashed into the bottle of sodium!

"Don't worry about this little spillage," said Charlie. "This is what a mop is for."

"No, Dad! That's sodium!" cried James. "Water will make it burst into ..."

But it was too late.

The mop was on fire!

The children all began to cheer.

"Cool!" said Norman.

"No!" said James. "This wasn't meant to happen."

The bunting had caught fire, too. The fire was spreading – and fast! Mrs Chen quickly got the children outside. It was time to call Fireman Sam!

The call came in at the Fire Station. Fireman Sam, Penny and Elvis put their helmets on and jumped into Jupiter.

ACTION STATIONS READY!

The volunteer firefighters jumped into Trevor's bus – this was their chance to help at a real fire!

"Hold on tight, everyone!" said Trevor.

When the Fire Crew arrived, the whole café was on fire! Sam and Elvis pulled on their breathing masks.

"I wonder what extinguisher they will use?" asked Dilys.

"I know!" said Trevor. "Because when in doubt ..."

"... you can fight fire with sand!" sang Trevor and Mike.

"You've got it!" said Elvis, picking up a bucket of sand.

Sam and Elvis ran into the café. The flames were getting higher. Elvis threw the sand on to the flames, then Sam blasted the flaming bunting with foam.

Soon, the fire was under control.

Everyone cheered when the fire was out.

"You were right, James," said Sarah. "Science is cool! Sorry for knocking over the sodium."

"That's okay, Sarah!" said James.

"Right, you two," said Fireman Sam. " I think next year you should have one party – a plain old party with balloons and party hats ..."

James and Sarah looked at each other.

"Nah! Boring!" they giggled.

COUNT ALONG WITH MANDY

Can you count the objects in the
boxes below? Point to the number
when you have added up each one!

1 2 3 4 5

SAM TO THE RESCUE

RESCUE AT SEA

Colour in this picture of **PENNY IN NEPTUNE.** You could draw some fish in the sea – or even a whale!

WHEEL-Y FUN WITH PAINT!

Fireman Sam loves travelling to emergencies in Jupiter. Trevor loves taking passengers all over Pontypandy in his bus. Tom loves racing to mountain rescues in his jeep.

Do you have any vehicle toys at home?

Then you can join Fireman Sam and friends with this messy, painty vehicle activity!

You will need:

A large sheet of paper
Bowls of different coloured paint
Small vehicle toys

What to do:

Simply dip the wheels of each vehicle toy in the paint. It makes it more fun if you use different colours. Then drive your vehicles all around the paper making wonderful wheel tracks as you go.

3,2,1 ... BLAST OFF!

James has drawn a rocket for his school project. Join the dots to make your own space picture then add lots of stars and a big moon!

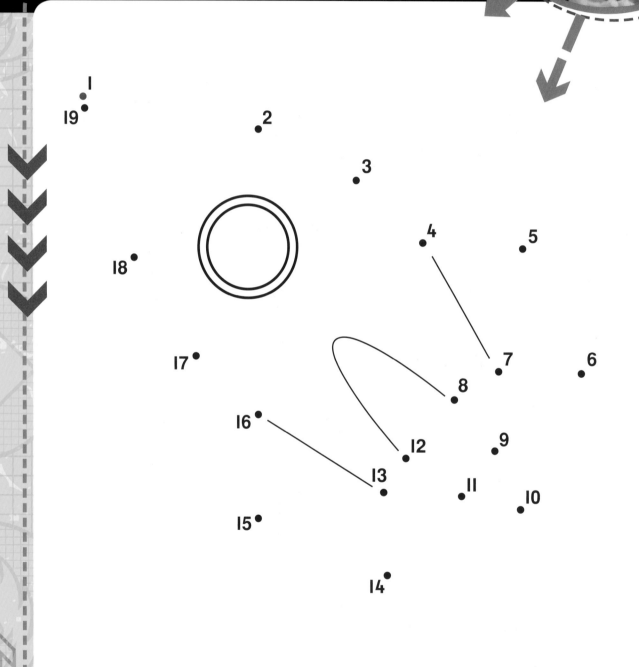

1
19
2
3
4   5
18
17   7   6
8
16   12   9
13
11   10
15
14

BLAZING MAZE!

A BBQ IS ON FIRE! Fireman Sam needs to act fast if he is going to put it out. Guide Sam through the maze to the fire, collecting the fire equipment along the way.

START ➡

FINISH

35

NEE NAH! NEE NAH!

Fireman Sam has a busy day ahead. There are lots of emergencies! Take Jupiter around Pontypandy by racing along the track with your finger.

Make sure you stop along the way to help Sam with his emergencies!

Officer Steele receives an emergency call. Moose is dangling from the lighthouse! Write over the numbers.

999

Who else is at the lighthouse?

Make a noise like a siren!

Moose holds on tight!

The Rescue Crew arrives. Which vehicle is used to save Moose?

Moose is pleased to be back on land! Now take Jupiter back to the Station!

NEW FRIENDS IN PONTYPANDY!

Some new friends have moved to Pontypandy! Everybody is very excited. Would you like to meet them?

The Sparkes Family

Joe Sparkes runs the garage and is great at fixing cars. He can be very silly, too. He loves doing what the kids do – skateboarding, go-karting – he'll try anything!

Lizzie Sparkes is Joe's wife and loves her new life in Pontypandy.

Hannah Sparkes is 11 years old and all the other kids love her. She is very funny and always comes up with the best ideas!

Ben Hooper

Ben is Pontypandy's new coastguard. He is a brilliant sailor and loves being out at sea. He likes to show off sometimes, but he is always on hand to help people in trouble. He's a top sea rescuer!

BEN TO THE RESCUE

The Sparkes family are drifting out to sea in a boat!
Guide Ben through the water maze to rescue them.
Make sure you don't bump into the rocks along the way!

START

FINISH

Answers on page 67.

CHARLIE'S BOAT

Charlie is telling Sarah and James all about his boat. Finish the activities so you can learn more, too!

2. Draw some fish for Charlie to catch.

1. How many people are in the picture?

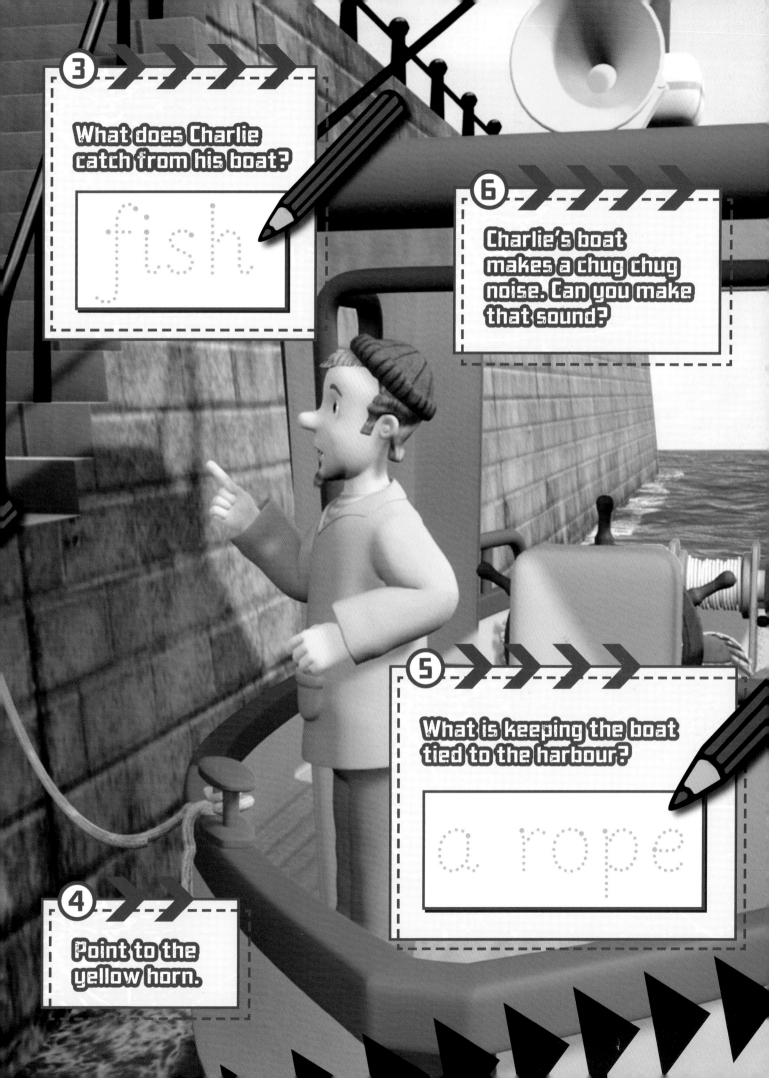

3 What does Charlie catch from his boat?

fish

6 Charlie's boat makes a chug chug noise. Can you make that sound?

5 What is keeping the boat tied to the harbour?

a rope

4 Point to the yellow horn.

How to play: Choose who is player 1 and who is player 2. Throw a dice and move in the direction of the numbers. If you land on an object, draw over it on your snowman. Keep going round and round until one person has collected everything they need to complete their snowman.

Pieces of coal for his eyes.

5

Carrot for a nose.

7

A big snowball for his body.

Player 1 snowman

Player 2 snowman

BEST SLEEPOVER EVER!

Norman was getting ready to go to a sleepover at Mandy's house.

"Have you packed my Army Bob pyjamas, mam?" asked Norman.

"Of course, everything is packed," said Dilys.

Just then, Norman heard a *TOOT! TOOT!* outside. It was time to go!

Dilys saw something on the floor – Norman's Army Bob pyjamas!

"Norman, wait!"

But it was too late. Norman had already gone – without his pyjamas!

At the Fire Station, Chief Officer Boyce had just arrived.

"What are you doing here, Sir?" asked Sam.

"Surprise Night-Shift Training Drills!" said Officer Boyce. "So you need to be on Red Alert."

Over at Mandy's house, Mandy and Sarah were in their pyjamas.

"It's a good job I don't have baby pyjamas like you!" said Norman. "Look at my Army Bob ..."

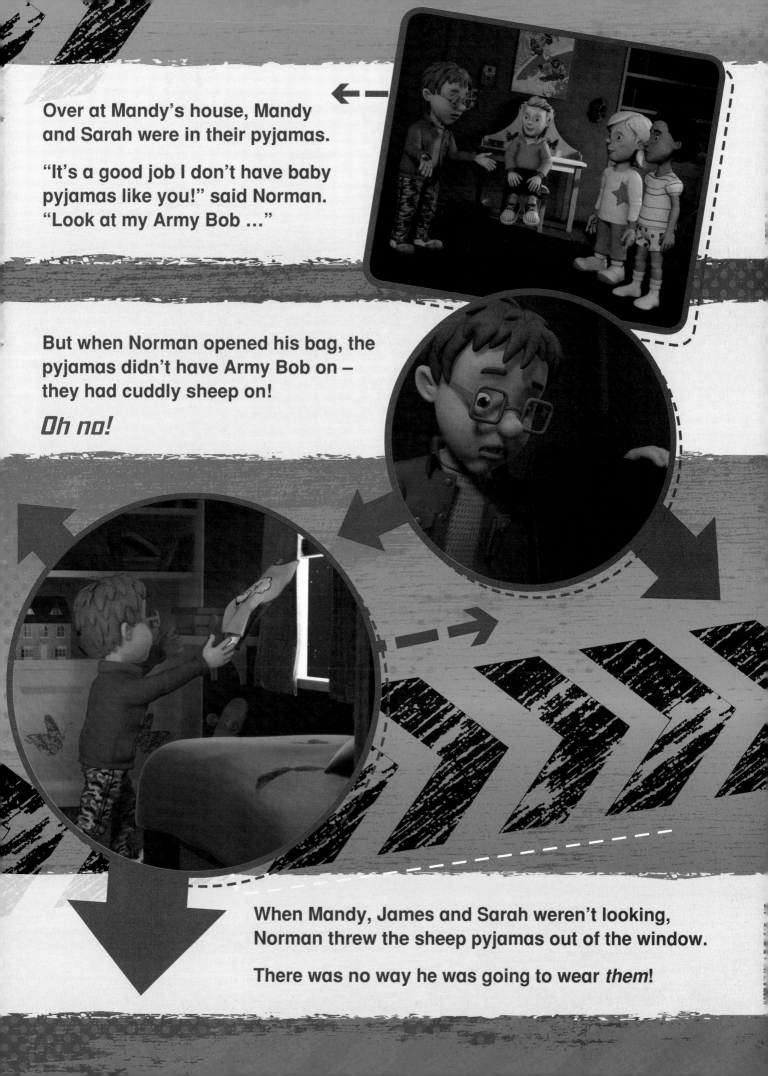

But when Norman opened his bag, the pyjamas didn't have Army Bob on – they had cuddly sheep on!

Oh no!

When Mandy, James and Sarah weren't looking, Norman threw the sheep pyjamas out of the window.

There was no way he was going to wear *them*!

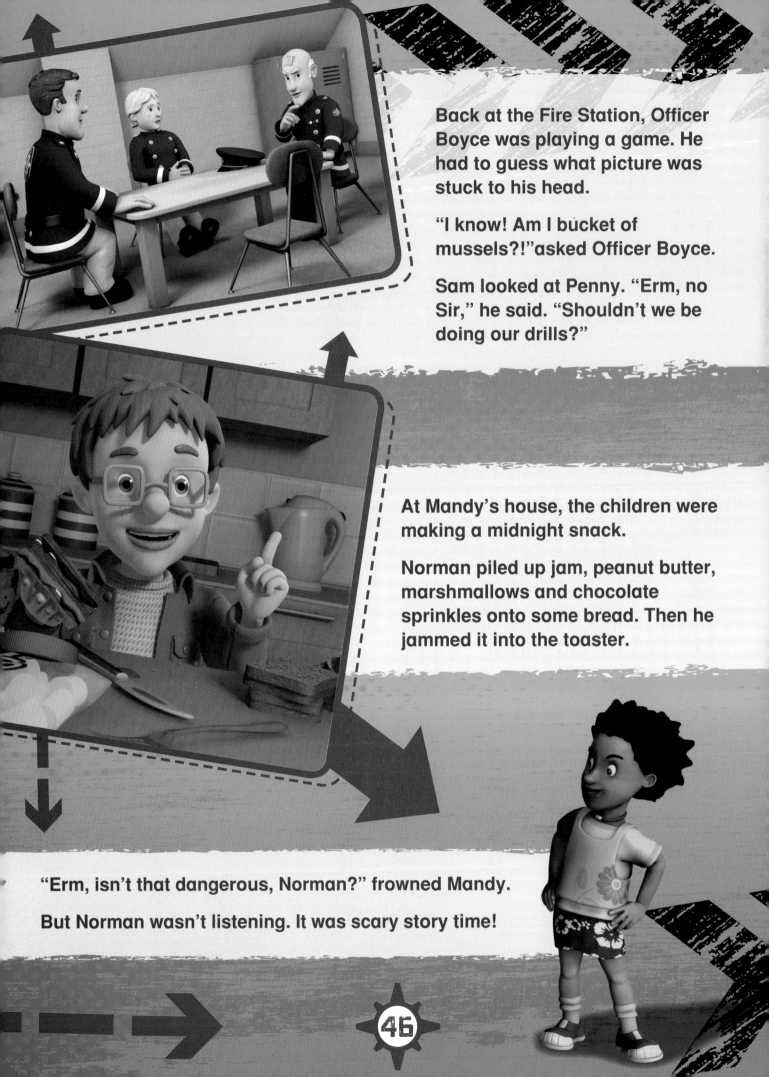

Back at the Fire Station, Officer Boyce was playing a game. He had to guess what picture was stuck to his head.

"I know! Am I bucket of mussels?!"asked Officer Boyce.

Sam looked at Penny. "Erm, no Sir," he said. "Shouldn't we be doing our drills?"

At Mandy's house, the children were making a midnight snack.

Norman piled up jam, peanut butter, marshmallows and chocolate sprinkles onto some bread. Then he jammed it into the toaster.

"Erm, isn't that dangerous, Norman?" frowned Mandy.

But Norman wasn't listening. It was scary story time!

The children went into the living room. Norman put on his spookiest voice.

"Welcome to the *Fog of Doom*. Once upon a time," began Norman. "There was a really scary person ... in a really dark wood ... with lots of fog ... ooooooohh!"

Suddenly James saw something misty under the door.

"Look, the fog from the story is coming through the door!" cried James.

But it wasn't fog. It was smoke. The toaster was on fire!

"Oh no!" said Norman. "We'd better call Fireman Sam. Quick!"

When the message came through to the Fire Station, Fireman Sam leapt into action!

"A fire at the Floods'," Sam said into his speakerphone. *"Everyone to Jupiter. Action Stations Go!"*

Jupiter raced off, with its siren blaring.

NEE NAH!

NEE NAH!

The fire at the Floods' was spreading – there was no time to lose!

When Fireman Sam arrived, smoke was pouring out of the Floods' house.

"It's in the kitchen, Sam!" said Norman.

Penny and Sam pulled on their breathing masks and ran into the house.

Penny turned off the electricity. Then Fireman Sam blasted the flaming toaster with his extinguisher.

They soon had the fire under control.

"I'm sorry," said Norman, sheepishly. "I put too much in the toaster."

"I hope you have learned that a toaster can be very dangerous if it's not used properly," said Fireman Sam.

Just then Fireman Sam spotted the pyjamas Norman had thrown out of the window.

"Erm, whose are these cuddly sheep pyjamas?" asked Fireman Sam. "Norman, they have your name inside …"

Mandy, James and Sarah burst out laughing. "Who's got the baby pyjamas now?!"

"Aww, this has turned into the worst sleepover ever!" said Norman.

"Wait!" shouted Officer Boyce. "I've got it! Am I a pair of trousers?"

"You are Sir … you are," smiled Fireman Sam.

RED ALERT!

UH OH! There are 3 emergencies in Pontypandy! Follow the trails to find out who is on their way to each emergency.

ⓐ

ⓑ

ⓒ

❶ There's a fire in Bronwyn's café!

❷

Naughty Norman is drifting out to sea!

❸ Moose and Tom are stuck up a tree!

Answers on page 68.

KITE COLOUR

The children are flying kites down by the sea. **Wheee!**
But somebody's kite is missing. Draw in the missing kite,
then use your **BRIGHTEST CRAYONS** to colour the picture.

SPOT THE DIFFERENCE

Jupiter is on the loose ... with Naughty Norman behind the wheel! Look carefully at these two pictures. Can you spot five differences in picture 2?

I

Colour in a badge each time you spot a difference!

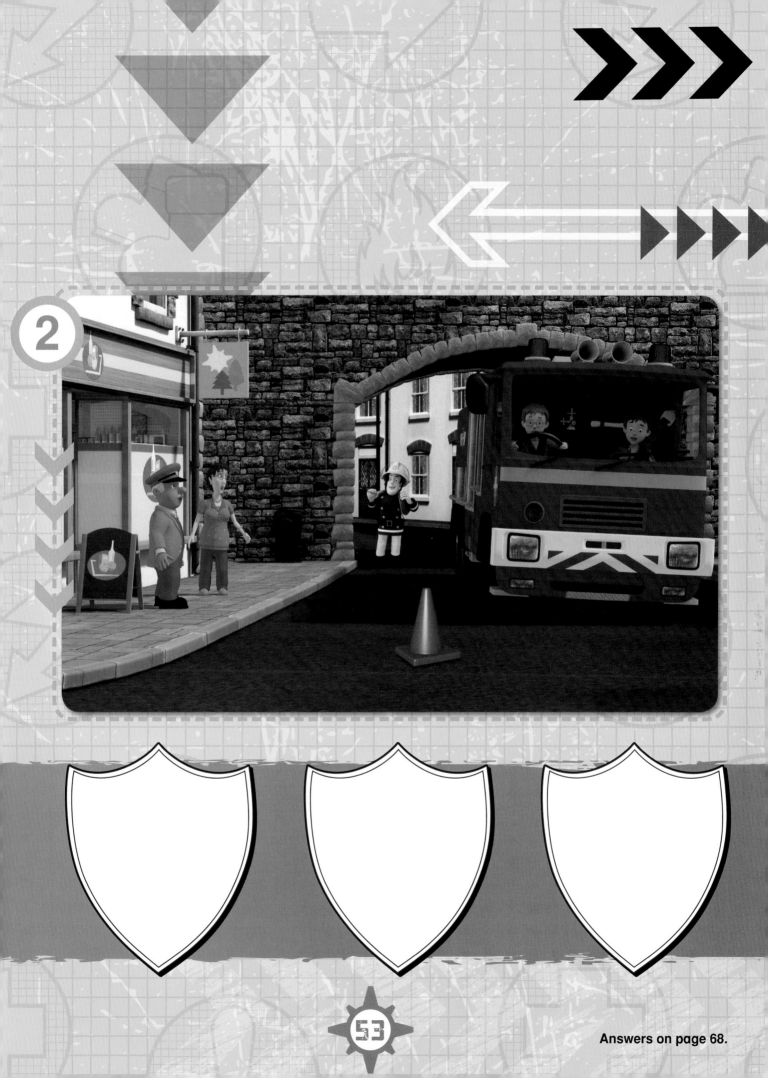

2

Answers on page 68.

PENCIL READY

Write over the letters below to discover things you'd see at Pontypandy Fire Station.

Somebody fetch me a pencil!

1. alarm

2. hose

3. helmet

4. engine

54

SHADOW MATCH!

Use a pencil to match up the Pontypandy friends with their shadows.

1

2

3

4

a

b

c

d

55

Answers on page 68.

EYE SPY

Norman loves to use his binoculars to find interesting things. Come and take a trip around Pontypandy to see what Norman has found.

①

Who is Norman looking at through his binoculars?

a

b

c

d

②

It's started to rain! Norman's binoculars have steamed up. Can you work out which animal Norman has spotted in the field?

Answers on page 68.

3

Ah, the sun is shining again and Norman has headed to the hills. There are lots of people about today. Can you spy the objects below?

 kite

 ball

 phone

 Norman's skateboard

THE PONTYPANDY POLAR BEAR

It was a snowy day in Pontypandy. Officer Steele was testing Saturn – a special flying thermal camera.

"Saturn can sense the heat from a body," said Officer Steele.

"Even if someone was *REALLY* cold?" asked Elvis.

"Yep, it could even find a human in the snow," said Officer Steele.

At the Wholefish Café, Charlie was reading The Pontypandy Post.

"The best photograph in the snow will make the front page of the newspaper," read Charlie.

"Let's take our camera out and take some snow pictures!" Sarah said to James. But James wanted to read his book about polar bears.

"We might find a real polar bear ..." said Sarah.

James suddenly looked up. "Let's go!"

Back at the Fire Station, the firefighters were taking it in turns to hide. Then they released Saturn to see if it could find them.

They were having a lot of fun with their new piece of equipment!

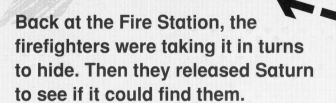

Meanwhile, Sarah and James were walking through the snow.

"I don't think we should go too far," said James, looking up at the snowy sky.

"Don't be a baby!" said Sarah.

Suddenly, Sarah noticed some footprints in the snow. They were huge!

"They might belong to a polar bear!" said Sarah, running after the footprints.

Sarah and James followed the footprints deep into the woods. It had started snowing again and the children were starting to feel cold and tired.

Sarah spotted a cave. "Let's wait in there until the snow stops. Then we can find the polar bear!"

"There is no polar bear," grumbled James.

At the Wholefish Café, Bronwyn was getting worried. It was getting dark and Sarah and James hadn't come home for tea.

Back inside the cave, James was grumpy.

"We shouldn't have come this far!" he said.

Just then, they heard a loud rustle outside.

"The polar bear!" they cried.

But it wasn't a polar bear – it was Moose! He had giant homemade snow shoes on.

"So it was your footprints in the snow – not a polar bear!" said Sarah.

Suddenly, there was a deep rumble. A sheet of snow fell over the cave and blocked the entrance. Moose, Sarah and James were stuck inside!

Meanwhile, Fireman Sam had received a call that Sarah and James were missing.

Sam, Elvis and Penny jumped into Venus.

"Don't forget to take Saturn," said Officer Steele. "It'll find them in no time!"

Saturn soon detected something deep in the woods. Penny checked the screen. She could see three figures.

"That could be them," said Penny. "But there's three of them!"

Sam headed towards the cave. He heard faint voices coming from inside the cave.

He quickly shovelled away some of the snow, and Sarah popped out!

Sam pulled Sarah and James out of the cave.

"It's all thanks to Saturn that we found you!" said Fireman Sam.

As he pulled Moose out, Sam slipped and fell into the snow with a THUMP!

Sam was covered in snow!

"You look like a polar bear!" giggled Sarah.

She quickly took a photo of snowy Sam.

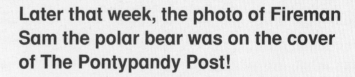

Later that week, the photo of Fireman Sam the polar bear was on the cover of The Pontypandy Post!

"You might not be a real polar bear, Uncle Sam, but you won the photo competition for us!" laughed Sarah.

"You always save the day – even when you fall in snow!" giggled James.

QUIZ TIME!

Now you have read The Pontypandy Polar Bear, see how much you remember about the story.

① What was the weather like in the story?

 ☐ **Sunny**

 ☐ **Snowy**

 ☐ **Foggy**

② What did James wear on his head?

 ☐ **A helmet**

 ☐ **A cone**

 ☐ **A woolly hat**

③ What did James and Sarah follow in the snow?

 ☐ **Footprints**

 ☐ **Torchlight**

 ☐ **Leaves**

4

Where did James and Sarah get stuck?

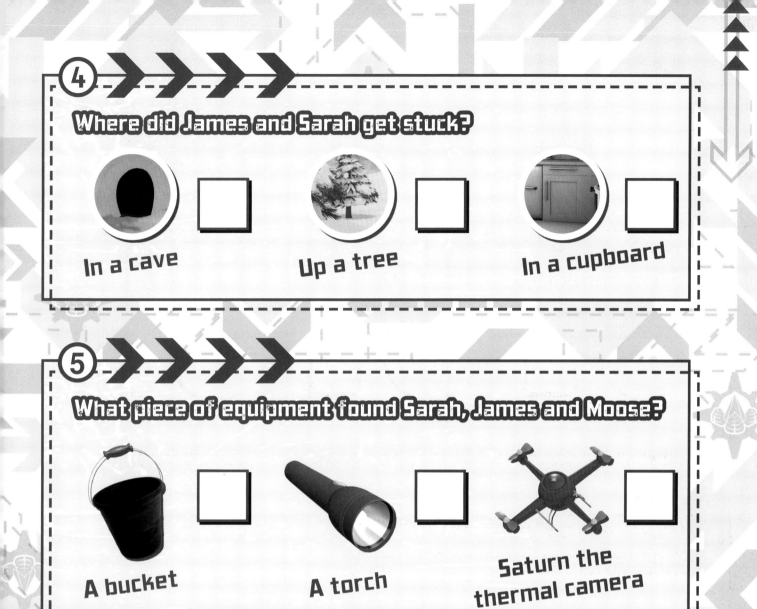

In a cave ☐

Up a tree ☐

In a cupboard ☐

5

What piece of equipment found Sarah, James and Moose?

A bucket ☐

A torch ☐

Saturn the thermal camera ☐

6

What photo won the newspaper competition?

Sam falling over! ☐

Sam as a polar bear! ☐

The firefighters flying Saturn ☐

65

Answers on page 68.

SEE YOU SOON!

IT'S TIME TO SAY GOODBYE!

Don't forget to colour the picture before you go!

P19 ODD ONE OUT
1. c, 2. d, 3. b, 4. a.

P35 BLAZING MAZE

P36 NEE NAH! NEE NAH!
Norman, Dilys, Mike, Mandy and Helen are at the lighthouse. Wallaby One is used to rescue Moose.

P39 BEN THE TO RESCUE

ANSWERS

P40 CHARLIE'S BOAT
1. There are 3 people in the picture.

P50 RED ALERT
a. 3, b. 1, c. 2.

P52 SPOT THE DIFFERENCE

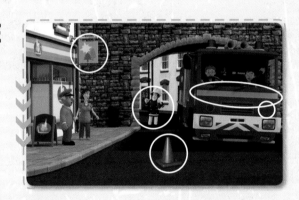

P55 SHADOW MATCH!
1. c, 2. d, 3. a, 4. b

P56 EYE SPY
1 a. Sam, b. Elvis, c. Dilys, d. Penny.
2 a sheep.

P64 QUIZ TIME!
1. The weather was snowy.
2. James wore a woolly hat.
3. James and Sarah followed footprints.
4. James and Sarah got stuck in a cave.
5. Saturn the thermal camera found Sarah, James and Moose.
6. Sam as a polar bear won the competition.

DON'T MISS FIREMAN SAM'S MAGAZINE!

IT'S FULL OF FIRE FIGHTING FUN!

Can you **find** all these Pontypandy pets on the page? **Circle** them when you **find** them.

How many pets are there?